G000163148

British Library Cataloguing in Publication Data

Newman, Nanette
  Archie.
  I. Title   II. Anderson, Susan
  823'.914 [J]   PZ7
  ISBN 0-340-39234-7

Text copyright © Bryan Forbes Ltd 1986
Illustrations copyright © Hodder and Stoughton Ltd 1986

First published 1986

Published by Hodder and Stoughton Children's Books,
a division of Hodder and Stoughton Ltd,
Mill Road, Dunton Green, Sevenoaks, Kent TN13 2YJ

Printed in Great Britain by Cambus Litho, East Kilbride

All rights reserved

Archie

Nanette Newman

Illustrated by
Susan Anderson

HODDER AND STOUGHTON
LONDON SYDNEY AUCKLAND TORONTO

I t was a warm summer day.
Archie climbed out of bed, tripped over his bed-socks, placed his glasses on the end of his nose and opened the window.
The sun was shining, the poppies nodded their red heads, the sky was the colour of forget- me-nots, and it seemed as if everything in the garden was smiling.
"Oh, my," said Archie - taking a deep breath and squinting into the sun -
"Oh, my, what a beautiful day for a Bear."
It was, in fact, a beautiful day for everyone, but that was what Archie said.

He dressed quickly, singing his favourite song, at first quite quietly, and then louder - and louder. When he reached the last note he jumped on to the bed and threw out his arms and his glasses fell off his nose.

"It's great to be a Bear,
On a lovely summer day.
It's great to be a Bear,
So that is why I say -
Oh, it's great to be a Bear,
Yes, it's great to be a Bear -
Yes, it's great to be a Bear -
Today.
Hurray."

It wasn't much of a song -
But then Archie wasn't much of a singer.

He danced around the kitchen, getting breakfast and bumping into things - filling his mug with an 'A' on it with milk, eating, singing, and spilling things, until finally he got hiccups and had to sit down. "Today," he said, "today is such a beautiful day, I ought to do something special." He thought for a minute, and held his breath to stop the hiccups. "I know. I shall celebrate. I shall make it a day to remember - I'll have a party - a Birthday Party," he said loudly, starting to hiccup again with excitement. "I shall celebrate this lovely day with a Special Birthday Party."

That settled, he rushed to the
telephone - knocking over his chair,
and slopping the milk out of the mug.
He rang his best friend, Jasmine Otter.
"Hello," said Archie. "Would you like to
come to a Birthday Party?"

"Is it your Birthday?" asked Jasmine.
"No, of course not," said Archie
"Then how can you have a Birthday
Party?" she asked.
"Well, it has to be someone's Birthday,"
said Archie.
"It's a silly idea," said Jasmine.

"Then you're not invited," said Archie, putting down the telephone.
"I don't care," he muttered . "I'll celebrate on my own."

T he rest of the morning he was very busy. The first thing he did was to get the book called:
'Everything A Busy Bear Needs To Know About Cooking'.
He turned to the page headed:-
'Recipes for Special Occasions'
and decided to make Best Bear Biscuits. In minutes the kitchen was in chaos. Archie became so covered in flour, he looked like a Polar Bear. The dishes and spoons piled higher in the sink, but this didn't worry Archie one bit. Eventually, after mixing and beating, rolling and

baking, the biscuits came out of the oven.
"Perfection," sighed Archie, well pleased
with his effort.

Next came the flowers. Archie picked daisies and dandelions (his favourites), placed them in a jug on the

garden table, and stood back to admire them.
"Now for the presents," he said.

He went to the desk, closed his eyes, opened the drawer, felt around, took something out, and (still with his eyes tight shut-no cheating) he wrapped the object in a piece of pretty wrapping paper. Only then did he open his eyes, so that he could see to tie the parcel up with a ribbon. He finished the whole thing with a big bow on top.

He then took some drawing paper out of his desk, drew a picture and coloured it in, and wrote 'Happy Birthday With Love' in big blue letters. He folded it carefully, and placed it in an envelope- and wrote S.W.A.L.K. (which, as everyone knows, means 'Sealed With A Loving Kiss').

He took this with the parcel and put them on the table next to the flowers.

Very soon everything was ready-the biscuits were laid out, with a candle on each one, some lemonade, and plum jam.

Archie changed into his best shirt- he brushed the fur round his nose until there wasn't a hair out of place. He then made a hat out of that morning's copy of 'Bears Bulletin' and, placing it on his head, he straightened his glasses and sat down at the table.

"What a day," he said to no one in particular. "What a superb day this is."

The sun shone even brighter, pleased to be appreciated.

At that moment a large fat Bee landed on the tip of Archie's nose. Archie was feeling so happy, he didn't bother to do anything about it, just let the Bee sit there, buzzing away.

Now the Bee was so used to being hit and swotted that she could hardly believe what was happening. Eventually she buzzed off Archie's nose and landed in the middle of a flower and looked at the Bear closely.

"Oh, my," said Archie. "What a delightful Bee you are. Would you like to share this Birthday Party?"

"Whose Birthday is it?" buzzed the Bee.

"I've no idea," said Archie, "but it must be somebody's, somewhere, don't you agree?"

"Too true, too true," said the Bee, liking this Bear immediately. "I'm happy to accept the invitation."

The party was a great success. The Bee (whose name was Matilda) was persuaded to try some plum jam. She had only had honey before. "I've never tasted anything so delicious," she said, diving on to the spoon for the third time.

Archie carefully lit the candles, and sang 'Happy Birthday' in his loud, flat voice, and Matilda buzzed the tune, and they then blew out the candles together.

"Make a wish," buzzed the Bee.

"I wish," said Archie, his shirt covered in biscuit crumbs, "I wish that everyone could know how to be happy on a beautiful day like this."

"Agreed," said Matilda, now sitting in the jam spoon, with plum jam on her head.

The card was then opened, and admired - "Now open the present," said Matilda.

"Isn't this exciting," said Archie, as Matilda placed herself on top of his hat to get a better view.

He undid the ribbon carefully, then unfolded the paper to reveal a rather sticky boiled sweet.

"Oh, my," he exclaimed in surprise - "isn't that a beautiful sight, round and red, and looking like a jewel in a King's crown. And also," he said sniffing, "smelling just like wild strawberries."

They both admired the sweet together, and when the sun disappeared, and the flowers nodded off to sleep, Archie and Matilda both knew they would be friends for ever.

That night Archie got ready for bed,
and put his paper hat on the
dressing-table. He left the red sweet on the
window-sill so that Matilda could enjoy it
whenever she wished.

He wound the ribbon around his ear, and took a piece of his best writing paper and wrote, 'Thank you so much for a wonderful Birthday Party'.
He folded it in four and put it by his bed, to read when he woke up in the morning.
He snuggled down under the patchwork quilt.
"Thank you," he said with a big smile on his face.
"Thank you *so much* for a truly beautiful Birthday Day."